The Mystery Of Covid-19

By Pamela Hillan
&
Penelope Dyan

Bellissima Publishing, LLC Jamul,
California
www.bellissimapublishing.com

Front Cover photo is from CDC Public Domain

IBSN 978-1-61477-467-9
First Edition

"Cowards die many times before their deaths. The valiant never taste of death but once."

William Shakespeare

Julius Caesar Act II, Scene 2

About The Book

Jan and Jenny are at it again! They want to save the world! And they are out to do that by sewing one mask at a time, and more. But then . . . something else happens when they decide to call their old friends Mr. and Mrs. Hufflefinger, retired CIA agents; and Jan and Jenny find out something about Covid-19 and the pandemic that it would be better (for them) if they did not know.

This is the thirteenth book in the Jan and Jenny mystery series. Written by award winning author, attorney, and former teacher, Penelope Dyan, and former court reporter, Pamela Hillan (who just happen to be life-long friends) just like Jan and Jenny, you are certain to enjoy this new adventure upon which the girls now embark.

Enjoy another Jan and Jenny mystery, as you travel through the pages of this sometimes spine tingling book; and find out exactly how Jan and Jenny actually deal with Covid-19, and why they are working unselfishly to help others during this very scary and difficult time.

And then . . . discover exactly why these two brave girls become suddenly very afraid.

The Mystery Of Covid-19

By Pamela Hillan
&
Penelope Dyan

CHAPTER ONE

Jan & Jenny's Command Center

Jan stared out her bedroom window and watched the rain falling from the dreary grey sky. She scratched her head, trying to brainstorm a way to save the world from the terrible pandemic, the dreadful Covid-19 virus. She soon realized that she desperately needed input from her best friend, Jenny, in order to have any success at a master plan for this journey. Grabbing her new cell phone, which she had received as a Christmas gift from her grandmother, she quickly dialed Jenny's number. It took only one ring before it was answered by her loyal friend, Jenny.

"Thank goodness you answered, Jenny! We absolutely must do something about this terrible pandemic situation before it's too late! Have any ideas off the top of your head?" Jan queried.

Jenny was completely silent (for too long in Jan's mind); but then she (somewhat scolding) responded, "Jan, we are *only kids.* What can we *possibly* do to help?"

Jan distraughtly replied, "Where there's a will, there's a way, Jenny! I just *know* we can figure *something* out if we just put our heads together."

"But absolutely everything is closing down around us!" Jenny exclaimed. "So when and where can we possibly even meet to devise a game plan?"

Jenny closed her eyes to concentrate for a few moments, to think about a secret meeting spot.

"I know," Jenny finally replied. "Remember that old red camper that my parents have had for years on the back of our property? Let's make that our command center! It hasn't been used in ages, but I'm sure it's a safe and secluded place for us to work our magic!"

Jan was so excited upon hearing this.

"That sounds perfect, Jenny! Our very own command post! Awesome! I'll get some food supplies and stuff together to keep us fortified. You get the needed 'okay' and I'll meet you there!" Jan said. And then she added, "But when will that be?"

"I'll get back to you on that, Jan. Just get prepared. This is a big job to tackle, girlfriend!"

Then Jenny went straight to her mom to butter her up for the plan she and Jan had in store for herself and Jenny. Luckily, as it turned out, since Jan and Jenny had so many successful results with their previous endeavors, Jenny's mom had no hesitation in allowing the girls to use the camper as their secret command center. And . . . maybe . . . just maybe . . . the girls could come up with a solution to this terrible pandemic, after all.

"Who am I to argue with success," Jenny's mother mused as she went back to her sewing machine. "Besides, they can't get into too much trouble in that old camper."

CHAPTER TWO

Setting Up Command Center 001

Jenny walked past her backyard swimming pool, out to the far-left corner of their property where the old camper was propped up by cement blocks and what appeared to be a great deal of two by four boards. She hoped that the camper was safe. It looked a bit precarious as it sat there propped up by what *she* viewed as a bunch of sticks and stones. But . . . her mom had set it up, and Jenny figured it would be safe, since her mom did the propping up of the thing. (The truth was that her dad *did* make beautiful music with his trumpet, but he couldn't seem to hammer a nail straight into anything, not *even* to hang a picture on the wall.)

Jenny's mom, on the other hand, was a sort of jack of all trades. She often told Jenny how she had helped her father (Jenny's grandfather) plumb the house and pull the wires for the electricity of their home back in Rhinelander. She loved to tell her how her grandmother's toilet consisted of an outdoor outhouse (that still happened to be on the property back home in Rhinelander) and how her grandmother used pages taken from the Sears Roebuck Catalog to wipe her bottom . . . that is (of course) until the Rhinelander paper mill started producing toilet paper. And since Jenny's great grandfather *happened* to work at the Rhinelander Paper Mill, *their* family was one of the very *first* families on the block to actually have access to something to which Jan and Jenny were quite accustomed, toilet paper!

Jenny wondered what all the fuss was about now with the whole toilet paper hoarding thing. Of all the things to be concerned about, why was toilet paper so important to today's Americans?

"It seems to me," she told Jan when she called her on the phone, "that toilet paper, and the having of it, should be way down on our country's list of concerns."

Jan agreed, of course.

"So . . . is everything 'A-Okay' for the use of the camper as our headquarters?" Jan asked.

"Come on up!" Jenny told her, grateful that at least this time Jan would be walking the mile up to *her house* and *not* the other way around!

"Meet me at the half-way point?" Jan asked.

Jenny sighed, because she *didn't* relish making that walk. It was cold outside, and the weatherman said rain was coming.

"I'm bringing brownies," Jan told her. "Do you have milk?"

"I think so," Jenny said.

"Then I do believe we are a go for today," Jan replied. "I'll grab my coat and leave right away, okay?"

"What do you think we can do, Jan?" Jenny asked sheepishly. "Do you have any ideas?"

"Well, I guess we can start by making a plan to help others in need. Then we can go from there."

"Sounds good to me!" Jenny said excitedly. "You know I'm a bit of a sucker for doing good."

"Let's face it, Jenny," Jan laughed; "you're just a goody two shoes!"

"It takes one to know one," Jenny replied, with cell phone in hand and on speaker, as she reached for her jacket.

"I'm going to meet Jan at the half-way point!" Jenny shouted to her mom, as Jenny headed for the front door.

"You two be very careful now!" Jenny's mom shouted back. "And don't talk to any strangers!"

"We won't!" Jenny yelled, as she headed for the front door.

Jan headed up the hill with a sack of brownies in hand and a backpack on her back.

"No one will miss these," she thought. "Anyway, I *did* bake them. And I *did* leave some in the pan."

CHAPTER THREE

Helping Others

Helping others was starting to look a little more difficult than it seemed! And Jan huffed and puffed (and grumbled) because she had to walk the *whole mile* up the steep hill to meet Jenny halfway, her head mostly looking down at the ground. But she figured all the effort would be worth it in the end, even if she and Jenny only ended up helping one person.

Jan finally glanced up and stopped counting the cracks in the sidewalk; and (as promised) there was Jenny coming down the hill to meet her. Now it didn't seem so tiresome. She had her best friend coming to meet her!

Upon seeing how tired Jan was when they reached one another, Jenny exclaimed, "Wow, Jan! You look pooped! Let me carry your backpack for you!"

Without hesitation, Jan handed her backpack over to Jenny.

"Good grief!" Jenny exclaimed. "What in the world do you have in there? I thought you said 'brownies'. I know brownies don't weigh *this* much!"

Jan smiled her big, friendly smile and laughed.

"You know me better than that, Jenny! The brownies are in the paper bag I'm carrying! They're not *even* inside the backpack! I came prepared to start saving the world from this pandemic! Just wait 'til we get to our command post, and I'll show you the cool stuff I have!"

Jenny shook her head in disbelief and giggled.

"You do amaze me, Jan. You're always thinking one step ahead. I'm sure glad we met each other. I think we're a good team!"

"Me too," Jan replied. "But let's just get to the command center!"

That said, the two girls started walking forward to Jenny's backyard and the camper, keeping their conversation to a minimum to conserve their energy.

When they finally arrived at Jenny's house, Jenny told Jan she had to close her eyes; and she would lead her to the command center. Jan complied, just wanting to sit down and rest her tired feet and exhausted body after her long uphill walk.

"Okay, Jan. You can open your eyes now," Jenny said, with excitement in her voice as they reached the camper.

When Jan opened her eyes, her mouth dropped. Then she squealed with joy and jumped up and down, clapping her hands!

"This is perfect!! Great job, Jenny!" she exclaimed.

Jenny had made a big command center sign out of some old barn wood, and she'd decorated it with bright paint and a little bedazzling! It looked awesome! It even had mini Christmas lights lit up around it! Now it was time to get to work!

CHAPTER FOUR

The Oh So Heavy Backpack

"So . . . whatever do you have in that backpack, Jan?" Jenny asked teasingly, as she handed the backpack back to Jenny.

"You will never, ever guess," Jan told her, as Jenny opened the door to the camper for the two of them to go inside it.

"Brawn before beauty," Jenny laughed, as she gestured for Jan to climb the camper stairs and to go inside.

"Well, somebody has to do the heavy lifting," Jan joked back, laughing.

"Mom turned on the electricity in here," Jenny said. "And so we have a fridge, and I put a quart of milk inside of it! I Hope that's enough milk to go with all those brownies!"

Jan set her backpack down on the camper couch.

"Are you going to tell me what you have in that backpack?" Jenny asked.

"Maybe," Jan teased.

"But you did bring the brownies, right? They're in the bag in your hand like you said, right?"

"Of course I did, Jenny! We girls on a mission have to keep up our strength!"

Jan held up the bag of brownies in her hand; and walked them over to the table, as Jenny wondered about what was in that *bulging* backpack.

"Okay, Jan . . . so exactly *what* do you happen to have inside that bulging backpack of yours?"

'Stuff," Jan replied. "Just stuff."

"What kind of stuff?"

"Lots of *very* heavy stuff . . . I have a lot of *very* heavy stuff in there," Jan told her.

"Well, I could tell *that* by all the sweating you were doing when you were climbing up the hill," Jenny quipped back. "So . . . *what* is in the backpack?"

"If I tell you, I might have to kill you," Jan told her, jokingly. "You know, like 007, and all that," she added affecting a British accent as she spoke.

Jenny laughed.

"Okay . . . Okay . . . I haven't forgotten your English roots, or even your Billy the Kid roots. But we need to get serious, Jan. This *is* a pandemic. People *are* being ordered to self-isolate. We haven't had *anything* like *this* happen since the great pandemic of 1918, during World War I. They estimate that 500 million people became infected in *that* pandemic, one third of the world population at that time; *and* they also estimate that 50 million people died worldwide in the 1918 Pandemic, with 675,000 deaths in the United States alone!"

"And that is *exactly* why my backpack is so heavy," Jan told Jenny, in all seriousness.

"Okay, Jan . . . So *exactly* what do you *have* in that bulging backpack of yours?"

"Just you wait and see," Jan told her teasingly. "Just you wait and see!"

CHAPTER FIVE

All The Goodies

After munching down a couple of the delicious triple chocolate chunk brownies Jan had made (with a nice glass of ice-cold milk) the two girls were ready to explore the contents of Jan's backpack. And Jenny was beside herself! She just couldn't wait!

So . . . Jan grabbed her extremely heavy backpack and lugged it over to the small table inside the camper and unzipped the first section.

"Get ready," Jan teasingly whispered as she ever so slowly pulled out the first of many items.

First . . . came a big bag of rubber bands. Jenny looked confused.

Then . . . out came a pack of coffee filters. Now Jenny was even more confused, but she kept silent, waiting for the rest of the contents of the mysterious backpack to be displayed.

Next . . . was a hot pink stapler!

Jenny's mind was really wondering now.

"What in the world was this girl up to . . .?" Jenny thought.

Jan started to laugh at this point.

"Come on now, Jenny. Don't you have a clue?" Jan teased.

Then Jan pulled out a package of micro-filter cloth that her dad had just happened to have in his garage for a project on which he had just (luckily) started working.

"Now do you get it?" she queried of Jenny.

Finally, she pulled out a sheet of directions on how to make a face mask.

"Oh! I get it. Cool, Jan." Jenny replied. "We can use my mom's portable sewing machine, instead of trying to do this by hand. It will be faster and easier, don't you think?"

"Perfect! Great idea, Commander No.1," Jan jokingly responded. "They really need lots of these face masks out there. At least that's what I heard on the news."

"What's next?" Jenny asked with growing excitement.

Without saying a word, Jan pulled out a bottle of 99 percent rubbing alcohol, a *big* bottle.

"Well, no wonder your bag was so heavy!" Jenny exclaimed.

Jan giggled.

Next, out came another big bottle filled with aloe vera gel, and a plastic bowl, a funnel, and a mixing spoon!"

"I know what this is for!" Jenny exclaimed with confidence in her voice. "We're going to make hand sanitizer, aren't we?"

"That's right, girlfriend!" came Jan's response.

Then she pulled out a recipe for making hand sanitizer, along with five extra large plastic bottles to which Jenny quickly added, "My mom has some essential oils and glycerin we can use too, to add fragrance and a hand softening agent. "

Jan was really starting to get into it now.

Then she pulled out a small bottle of tea tree oil, and exclaimed with excitement in her voice, "I was thinking the very same thing! This is going to be so much fun! We will have our own mini laboratory!"

Having emptied the bag of *most* of its contents, Jan and Jenny smiled at each other and sat down to start planning their strategy for hopefully ending the corona virus pandemic.

The only things left in the bag were Jan's overnight essentials and some clean clothes. You see, it was a given that she would be spending a few days at Jenny's house. They always stayed at either Jenny's house or Jan's house when they were working on one of their projects.

Jenny turned on the portable TV she'd set up in the camper. They were attached to cable programming, as well as to the wireless internet, now essentials in their business of saving the world.

And yes, they *were* out to save the world again; and this time it was going to be a *very* big save, even if right now it was simply one baby step at a time.

Jan grumbled with impatience at the thought of all those baby steps. She wanted to get where she was going; and she did not *like* climbing hills, as everyone well knew.

"Every journey begins with one step," Jenny told Jan, trying to ease Jan's anxiety over this particular project.

"I guess for now it's shelter in place," Jan replied. "So, we may as well get cooking!"

"Speaking of cooking," Jenny interjected, "we'll be going into the house for dinner."

"Can we make grilled cheese sandwiches and tomato soup?" Jan asked, licking her lips with the tip of her tongue.

"I guess so," Jenny told her. "Mom's at work right now, so I'm doing the cooking again."

"Oh, goodie!" Jan exclaimed.

"But let's keep those delicious brownies out here for us," Jenny told her. "We have ice-cream inside for dessert."

"That's good thinking, Jenny; because we are going to be up late tonight working on all of this stuff; and we'll need our nourishment."

"And we'll be planning our next moves, Jan. Don't forget that!"

"And, as usual, I'm sure we will have some moves to make," Jan giggled. "After all, you *can't* save the world all at once, Jenny!"

"But just maybe we can save the world, one step at a time," Jenny added. "Just maybe we can save the world one step at a time."

CHAPTER SIX

It's All About The Trumpet

Jan and Jenny shortly thereafter proceeded to the house kitchen, leaving the backyard camper vacant for the moment, knowing they would return after dinner to work again on the projects Jan had laid out for them. Jenny went straight to the cupboard, and got out the large can of tomato soup and mixed it together with the required corresponding can of milk, while Jan got out the bread and American processed cheese slices and built the sandwiches.

"Do you think ten sandwiches will be enough?" Jan asked.

"Better make it an even dozen just to be safe," Jenny told her. "My brother eats a lot, and six of us will be sitting down to eat."

"Your dad's going to be home?" Jan asked.

"Yes. Trumpet lessons aren't considered an essential service, and so he can't leave the house for that; but he'll be giving virtual trumpet lessons on the internet . . . well, not *exactly* virtual lessons, I guess he'll be doing them by Skype."

"It sounds like a plan," Jan replied.

Jenny smiled as she set about making the tomato soup.

"Are you guys going to be okay over this?" Jan asked. "Since my dad's in the Navy, he'll probably be called up to do emergency services," Jan added, as she continued to build the sandwiches.

"Oh, yeah . . . we'll be fine. My dad has a morning television gig, and television is an essential service now. He and three other guys will be playing for a local morning show that hopes to go into syndication. And he has a recording contract in Los Angeles that guarantees him his wages whether or not any recording is made or distributed. And he has a recording gig here too, a virtual thing."

"That's good."

"I'll say . . . because there are no gatherings of more than ten people allowed anywhere right now, so that means no live music in restaurants or clubs. Everyone has to be creative under these new 'stay in place' orders," Jenny added, as she stirred the pot of creamy tomato soup now cooking on the stove.

"Life is great, don't ya think, Jenny?"

"I guess so."

"Do you think we'll be famous singers some day?"

"Whatever made you ask that right now, Jan?"

"I don't know. We sing. And we have fun singing together; and we could be like the Lennon Sisters or the Maguire Sisters, except that we would be a duet!"

"Well, my dad said if we could get a barbershop quartet together, he could get us some work," Jenny told Jan, as she took the bubbling, creamy tomato soup off of the hot burner, and put it on a hot-pad on the table, and proceeded to set the table for dinner.

Jan got out the butter and began buttering the soon to be grilled cheese sandwiches.

"Do you really think we could get work if we made ourselves into a quartet?" Jan asked.

"Well, if my dad didn't mean it, he wouldn't have given me all of those books of music that have musical barbershop quartet arrangements in them for the female voice!"

"Where will we get two more people to sing with us?" Jan asked.

"Well, we can always ask my sister. She's younger, and she'd fit the bill for the cute factor. And she really *can* sing! And she hears harmonies really well."

"As good as you do?" Jan asked.

"Maybe even better," Jenny said, with all seriousness. "Her voice isn't exactly developed, but she sure can sing harmony; and she's cute, and she's a natural!"

"That just might work! Then we'd have three, and we'd only need a fourth! But first things first, Jenny . . . first, we have to save the world!"

"And before that we have to eat dinner!" Jenny added with a smile.

And so soon thereafter, Jan and Jenny, and Jenny's sister, brother, mother and father . . . all sat down at the kitchen table to eat.

"Do you think people spend too much time obsessing about food?" Jenny asked her father.

"Only if they're hungry," her father replied. "Only if they're hungry," he repeated.

And . . . that was all that was said on that particular subject, on that particular night, at the dinner table.

CHAPTER SEVEN

Back At The Command Center

After Jan and Jenny finished clearing the table and washing the dishes, they announced that they would be working in the trailer to come up with some ideas for helping the medical professionals on the front lines who were trying to combat the Covid-19 pandemic. According to the television news, there was a shortage of protective gear and sanitation supplies in both hospitals and nursing homes. They wanted to play a part in fighting this terrible disease that was crippling the world population, and they thought they had some good ideas to help save the world! And they *knew* this had to be done in steps.

So, without any further hesitation, out the backdoor they flew, running as fast as they could to 'The Command Center'.

Once inside the old camper, and a bit out of breath, Jenny picked up the instructions for making the face masks; and Jan headed to where she had set out the supplies for mixing the hand sanitizer on the front counter.

"I brought these five extra-large clear plastic empty bottles for the hand sanitizer part of this project," she said, as she rearranged the bottles and mixing supplies she had earlier placed on the small kitchen counter. "We'll deliver in bulk and then hospital and nursing home staff can refill all their empty sanitizers' . . . you know, the ones they have outside hospital and nursing room doors."

"Sounds like a plan," Jenny said with a smile.

Jenny *always* liked to have a plan!

Jan grabbed a couple cans of soda from the mini-fridge and joined Jenny at the table. (Jenny was pleased her mother had been so thoughtful, putting soda in the mini-fridge for them to drink,)

Jan handed Jenny one of the cans of soda.

"Thanks," Jenny said, as she popped the can open and took a big gulp of soda. "From the looks of these instructions, I think we will be up all night if we want to make any progress at all, Jan."

"Well," Jan began . . . "we can cut the patterns from the special micro-filter cloth and assemble them tonight; and in the morning, you can get the portable sewing machine; and you can start sewing the masks together, while I mix the hand sanitizer. And . . . by the way . . . my dad said this material is almost as good as the material used in the real N-95 masks that the doctors have been using in the intensive care units. It was created for the astronauts to use at the space station!"

"Sounds like a plan," Jenny said, noting she was repeating herself by saying something she had previously said. And then she added, "If what your dad said about this stuff is true, that's really awesome!"

Now it was Jan's turn to smile.

. "We need to use special care in cutting the materials to keep them sterile," Jenny continued. "There's a clean white sheet above your head in the cabinet. That should keep things sanitary. My mom bleaches everything that's white, and she just washed those sheets."

"Good idea," Jan retorted. "And I also brought two boxes of latex gloves for us to use to keep things clean and sterile, and to deliver with the masks!" Jan said, as she went to her now not so bulging backpack and pulled out a box of 100 pairs of latex gloves.

"You think of everything, Jan! How many masks do you think we can make? I just heard on the news that they are desperate for these things, and that they will need millions of masks and other protective gear before this thing subsides."

Jan looked up at Jenny with a hopeless look on her face.

"Well," Jan sighed, "let's just do the best we can. I doubt very much that we could *ever* make a *million* masks. We'd have to work night and day for *years* to make a million masks!"

The girls looked at each other and chuckled, and then they gave each other a grand high-five hand gesture.

And then Jan added another interesting tidbit.

"I have a great idea where we can take this stuff, or send it, if we can't leave here."

"And where is *that* pray tell?" Jenny asked.

"I went on the Internet, and there were a couple of nursing homes that were in dire need of protective gear and what not. I thought that would be perfect! We can chose one of them, and make our delivery," Jan said, as she gazed toward Jenny with a quirky little grin; and she could see that Jenny absolutely loved *the* idea!

(But Jan was saving the best for last!)

"I'm getting more excited by the minute!" Jenny squealed.

"I'm so glad you're this excited. Because I think I know just the place!" Jan told her. "There's a really nice nursing facility for the old folks in La Jolla. They even have a fabulous ocean view! And I think some very important people reside there, too!"

"Oh, Jan, you never cease to amaze me! You always make our projects full of fun and excitement! I can hardly wait."

"Well, just keep it in mind that we may not be able to actually go inside or even distribute the masks in person. We're more than likely have to overnight this stuff to them (with their permission) or do a curbside or front door drop," Jan explained.

"That works for me," Jenny said.

"It works for me too!" Jan happily exclaimed, as the two of them sat down at the table and got right to work.

CHAPTER EIGHT

When I'm Sixty-Five!

"What do you think we'll be like when we're sixty-five?" Jenny asked, as the girls ever so carefully piled up the ready to sew parts for their sixty-fifth mask.

"I don't know, Jenny. But right now, my hand is cramping up from all the pattern cutting," Jan told her, wryly adding, "I guess we won't make a million masks tonight."

"I never said we would make a million masks tonight, Jan. I just said I heard on the television that they *needed* a million masks," Jenny laughed. And then she added, "Do you know what my dad would say about that? .

"No," Jan replied. "What would your dad say?"

"He would say, or rather he would ask, 'Who are *they*', and then he would tell me to gather all the facts before I made such a supposition. Of course, that would be after I told him that I didn't know who 'they' were!"

Jan laughed.

"Your dad's smart, Jenny."

"I know, and my mother doesn't even call him a smart ass."

"Watch your tongue, Jenny."

"Well, I can't help it that I'm smart, and neither can you."

"I'm not so smart, Jenny."

"Yes, you are! Just look at all this stuff you've assembled."

"I'm just efficient and well-organized. That's all, Jenny! I'm just efficient and well-organized!"

"I wish I could be as well-organized as you are, Jan. Your dresser drawers are absolutely, perfectly organized, not to mention your 'everything has a place, and everything is in its place' closet! Half of my stuff is stuffed under my bed! I have shoes under my bed that I haven't worn in years! I have shoes under there that are two sizes too small!"

"Well, maybe when we're done saving the world again, I can help you get organized, Jenny."

"Do you mean it, Jan?"

"Do I have blue eyes and blond hair, Jenny?"

"Yes."

"Then I mean it!"

"Now what does having blue eyes and blond hair have to do with meaning anything, Jan?

"I don't know. I just thought it sounded funny."

"Do you mean *you* were being a smart . . ."

"Don't say it, Jenny," Jan said interrupting her. "You know it *isn't* ladylike."

"But I'm no lady," Jenny scoffed. "I'm just a kid."

"Keep telling yourself that, Jenny," Jan laughed. "Just keep telling yourself that."

"Well, I'm not sixty-five," Jenny told her. "At least I'm not sixty-five yet."

"Hmmm," Jan mumbled as she paused for a moment and rubbed her sore hand. "Do you think we should sing that Beatles song, 'When I'm sixty-five" for the old folks at the nursing home?"

"It might make them sad," Jenny said, brow furrowed.

"Why?" Jan asked.

"Because they're probably *all* way over the age of sixty-five, Jan. It might make them sad if they think about it."

"I don't get it Jenny, why?"

"Because the song says, 'Will you still love me? Will you still need me, when I'm sixty-five?' And that might get them thinking about being alone."

"But they won't be alone if we are there, Jenny."

"I don't think it will be possible to go inside the nursing home, Jan. Right now even family is prohibited from visiting them."

"But we *are* doing something nice."

"I think there are plenty of songs we can do, Jan. And we can maybe Skype and sing later on; but maybe we just shouldn't sing that song."

I guess you're right, Jenny," Jan replied; and then she quickly changed the subject and somewhat randomly said, "I sure could go for another soda and some tortilla chips!"

"Coming right up," Jenny said, as she got up and retrieved two more sodas from the fridge and reached up and took down a huge bag of tortilla chips from the cupboard. "My mother also thinks of everything," Jenny said, as the two of them moved over to the small sofa area to eat and drink, protecting the 'clean' area where they were working.

"Let's watch some late-night TV," Jenny said, with the television remote in hand; "or is it time for early morning TV now?"

"Who cares?" Jan asked kiddingly. "My hand hurts and we need a break."

"Maybe you should ice it," Jenny offered.

"Nah, I'll be fine as long as I can grab those tortilla chips and drink this nice cold soda!" Jan quipped.

Then the girls laughed. It seemed those two girls always found the fun in things, even in the very worst of times. And this was one of those very worst of times.

CHAPTER NINE

When Everything Is Sew Sew!

"It seems like I have just been sewing forever and ever," Jenny grumbled as she stitched up the fiftieth mask.

"Well, not exactly," Jan laughed, carefully finishing up the final touches on the five extra-large bottles of hand sanitizer.

"Exactly how long is forever?" Jenny asked, as she reached for the material to begin mask fifty-one, setting mask fifty into the growing pile of masks sitting on the table next to the sewing machine.

Jan ignored the question.

"I think that it's my turn to sew now," she said. "Remember? We decided to change places every twenty-five masks, and you've sewn fifty! It's your turn to cut and assemble the parts into piles now."

"But . . . what about making the hand sanitizer, Jan?"

"I'm all finished with that, Jenny. I just now finished making it."

"Sorry, I didn't notice, Jan. I was too busy sewing, I guess," Jenny said, as she placed mask 51 into the growing pile of masks.

"We could make a lot of money if we sold these things door to door," Jan surmised.

"But that's not the point of us doing this," Jenny told her. "*And* . . . if we went door to door, we could be *exposing* ourselves to the virus."

"I guess so," Jan replied. "But I am really getting tired of all of this."

"Making the masks and the hand sanitizer?"

"No. I'm tired of having to stay inside day after day, after day! I thought they said kids were immune to this thing, Jenny."

"No, we *aren't* immune, Jan. We're just less likely to die of it. And *now* they're saying kids can get blood clots or something like that, and that the blood clots can go to our hearts. And who *knows* if this will damage us in the long run. I don't relish being an invalid in my old age, or even in my adulthood."

"Our adulthood will be old age," Jan replied, with a scowl on her face. "This is *supposed* to be the best time of our lives; and here we *are* isolating and making masks and hand sanitizer! We can't *even* watch a movie at the movie theater! Right now they're all closed!"

"And they say the virus may now be mutating, and that it can be transmitted more easily than before," Jenny went on, trying to fully explain her point of view.

"Oh yeah? More easily than before what, Jenny?" Jan asked, with a tone in her voice that was somewhat sarcastic.

"Before how the virus was transmitted before yesterday, and the day before yesterday," Jenny replied. "You heard what Dr. Fauci said on the news today, didn't you?"

"Oh yeah. He did say that."

"All we can do is what we can do, Jan."

"And it doesn't seem like much, Jenny."

"It's better than doing nothing at all, Jan. Some people aren't even bothering to do anything!"

"Well, it seems to me we can do more."

"We could visit the old lady up the street, Jan. She must be lonely. We haven't visited her in a long time."

"Okay," Jan replied. "And we can bring her a mask!"

"And some cookies!" Jenny exclaimed. "We can bake her some Covid-19 safe cookies."

"Do you think we should get tested first to make sure we are Covid-19 negative and don't have the virus?" Jan asked.

"I'll see what my mom can do. Maybe she can take us to one of those drive-up test places."

"Sounds like a plan, Jenny. I mean we are healthy and have no symptoms; but we still need to make sure we aren't carriers," Jan said, as the girls changed their workplace positions.

"Mask fifty-one coming up," Jan said, as she took her place behind the sewing machine.

"Actually, it's mask fifty-two," Jenny confessed. "I never stopped sewing while we talked. Take it as a sort of freebie," Jenny said, laughing.

"Oh my, now you have thrown off all of the numbers," Jan told her. "You know how pragmatic I am. I guess I will just have to change my entire mindset, Jenny."

"Just take it one step at a time," Jenny replied with a grin.

CHAPTER TEN

Let's Get Tested!

Jan and Jenny spent the rest of the day packaging the masks individually, along with a pair of disposable gloves in a Ziploc bag, to be distributed to any seniors they could reach. There were so many rules in place, because of the Covid-19 virus, that it was difficult to get your foot in the door to help; but they had a list of potential nursing homes willing to accept any help they could get. So that's where Jan and Jenny decided they would start. But first, they needed their Covid-19 tests to make sure they were not carriers of the virus.

"Hey, Jan, my mom just called, and she told me that they're giving free tests down at the local YWCA. Wanna go?"

"Of course I do! Do we need a parent's consent form?" Jan queried.

"My mom said she would take us if we get ready to leave right now. She's on her way home. She said that she checked with the YMCA, and she can give the okay for both of us. Then she's going to do a curbside pickup of the groceries she ordered on line."

That sounded perfect to Jan. Jenny's Mom was always so accommodating. She was a great mom.

Before they knew it, they were in Jenny's Mom's car and on their way to be tested! Jenny's dad would take the rest of the family.

"They stick that thing way up your nose, ya know," Jan said, looking a little frightened.

Jenny snickered.

"Oh, Jan, it can't be that bad! Just think of it as a service to our country to help others in need. And we can't complete our plan if we don't get tested and make sure we don't have the virus, or that we are carriers."

"Easy for you to say," Jan replied. "I don't like things up my nose!"

"Okay, girls," Jenny's mom interjected. "I'll go first so you can see how easy it is."

That seemed to satisfy both girls, and soon they were then pulling into the YWCA driveway.

"Look, girls!" Jenny's mom exclaimed. "You don't even have to get out of the car! Just stay calm; and it will be over in a flash!" Jenny's mom added, easing their anxiety.

And then before the girls knew it, the testing was completed; and they were on their way to the grocery store for the grocery curbside pick-up Jenny's mom had ordered.

How do you girls feel about having Tempura shrimp and rice for dinner?" Jenny's mom asked, as she pulled up into to space 3 of the curbside pick-up.

"Yummy!" Jan exclaimed.

"And I ordered some rocky road ice-cream for dessert," Jenny's mom added.

"Double yummy!" Jan exclaimed again.

Jenny's mom just assumed Jan would be staying for dinner, and she was right, as usual.

"I just love having dinner at your house," Jan said, as Jenny's mom dialed the number on the sign to announce her arrival for the scheduled curbside pick-up and pressed the button to pop open the trunk of the car.

The groceries were delivered, and Jan saw Jenny's mom had also ordered four twelve packs of soda, along with some tortilla chips. She couldn't see what else was being placed in the trunk of the car.

The masked and gloved delivery girl put everything inside the trunk, and then she shut the trunk of the car; and Jenny's mom gave her a thumbs-up. Then they headed back to Jenny's house.

"I trust that you girls will help unload the groceries and put them away for me while I start the dinner," Jenny's mom said as they drove.

"Of course we will!" Jan exclaimed, as Jenny grumbled under her breath.

Jenny thought her sister and brother should help with things for once in their lives, but she decided to keep her thoughts to herself and to keep the peace. Her father had, after all, told her to choose her battles carefully; and Covid-19 was enough of a battle in and of itself.

CHAPTER ELEVEN

The Protests!

“What do you think about the protests going on now?” Jenny asked as the two girls began putting the groceries away.

“Which protests?” Jan asked. “Are you talking about the protests against the police, or the protests against wearing masks?” Jan continued, having learned from Jenny to be reference specific, which Jenny was not exactly doing now.

“All of them,” Jenny told her.

Jenny’s mom continued to prepare the evening meal. Since she was a first generation, full-blooded Swede, she preferred to not have opinion about such things and felt she should be neutral at all times; because she was taught Sweden was *always* neutral. And this *was* true, because Sweden had a history of neutrality stretching back to the early part of the 19th century; and it had not been militarily occupied since 1523, or *even* at war since 1814. However, during the 17th century, Sweden was actually a major military power in Europe, and for a time it controlled Finland and Norway, not to mention the Swedish Vikings who had conquered Denmark and parts of Russia during its long history as a sovereign nation.

In any event, it gave Jenny's mom a reason not to think about or to get involved in such discussions; and she believed this made her life not only simpler, but also easier. So she changed the subject.

"Be sure to get that ice-cream into the freezer right away," she said.

Jenny, however, like her Italian father, was full of opinions about everything; and she was not afraid to voice her opinions, much to her mother's dismay.

"Well . . ." Jenny began, "I think protests that are peaceful are good. But I also believe history will show these particular protests to be ill-advised, because protestors are not taking proper precautions by wearing masks and self-distancing. And the protests against wearing masks have nothing to do at all with personal freedoms and are dangerous to everyone . . . *to humanity itself* . . . because these protests *are threatening* the health and well-being of the entire world! So I think it's just awful!"

"What can we do about it, Jenny?" Jan asked.

"I don't know. But I'm sure that we'll think of something, because we always do!" Jenny told her.

"Now you girls stay out of trouble," Jenny's mother said, as she prepared the rice in the rice cooker, and checked on the Tempura shrimp cooking in the oven at 400 degrees.

"Thank goodness for frozen food!" Jenny's mom exclaimed with a smile. And then she added, "What do you girls want for a vegetable?"

"I don't care," Jan told her, as Jenny realized her mother had once again succeeded in changing the subject.

"Now . . . wherever are your brother and sister?" Jenny's mom asked Jenny, as she took a package of frozen peas from the freezer.

"I'm not exactly my brother's keeper, or my sister's keeper," Jenny told her. "But I do suspect John is lying in front of the TV set watching a western, and Christine is outside doing cartwheels!"

"Don't you get smart with me!" Jenny's mother snapped back . "Go and find them, and tell them dinner is about to be served!"

At that moment, Jenny's dad walked through the front door and into the kitchen, all smiles.

"I'll get them," he said, winking at Jenny. Jenny and her dad had their own way of communicating. He understood her, even if her mother didn't. But then, again, maybe Jenny's mom understood more than she let on . . . she always seemed to have a trick up her sleeve, after all. Maybe Jenny just had a lot to learn. Jan seemed to get it, but Jan's mom was different.

She had a problem; and Jan had enough to do dealing with just that. The odd thing about it was that Jenny never knew Jan's mother drank too much, or that she neglected Jan and her little sister; because Jan hid it so well from the world. Jan was just a kid, after all, so what was *she* to do? All she could do was hide the problem and take care of her mother and sister the very best way she could. She wished her mom was like Jenny's, but she was smart enough to know she had to accept the cards she was dealt. And Jenny's house and all of their adventures and projects were a great escape for her. When Jan was home, she could think about all of that; and it gave her a small measure of solace.

"When do you think we will get the test results?" Jan asked Jenny's mom.

Jan, like Jenny's mom, was also very good at changing the subject, even if she was the one to start it. (It was a tactic Jenny never had seemed to learn.)

"They said we would get the test results tomorrow," Jenny's mom said, never acknowledging the girls were actually in the car when she was told that.

"Oh, goody!" Jan exclaimed. "Then we can get back to work helping people!"

Jenny nodded in agreement, as her mind swirled, thinking about what they could do and would do.

"Onward and upward!" Jenny exclaimed,

CHAPTER TWELVE

Shrimp And Rice, How Very Nice!

Once everyone was seated at the dinner table Jan suggested a prayer of thanks be said to the Lord for the meal they were going to enjoy together, and for humanity to have the wisdom to cope with Covid-19, the terrible pandemic plaguing the world at this time. Everyone held hands and prayed together. Afterward, they all felt relief, and hope for the future.

As the food was being passed around the table, Jan had a thought come to mind. So being a bit outspoken, as she was, she asked Jenny's dad a question.

"I know you like to play the trumpet with a band in nightclubs and such," Jan began, "and since everything has been basically closed down for group gatherings, how has that affected your profession?"

Jenny's dad glanced at Jenny's mom and smiled, amused such a question would even come out of such a young person. But then, while attempting to answer, he was interrupted by Christine, Jenny's younger sister, who began throwing a temper tantrum over peas being served, since she hated them so. And then she screamed at her brother, John, for mixing his rice and peas together.

"So much for a nice calm dinner conversation," Jan surmised; and then she just decided to eat her tempura, dipped in sweet hot sauce, and to ask her question another time.

Christine was scolded for being so disruptive at the table; but the mood had then changed so drastically that everyone just ate as fast as they could, so that dinner would be over with and done! Good old Christine once again managed to ruin the moment, a trait she was perfecting with some regularity!

Jan and Jenny just looked at each other, shrugging their shoulders and finished dinner without further conversation.

Jenny's dad excused himself from the table and went into the bedroom, from where you could hear him playing his trumpet. That was his way of relieving stress, and he was really good at playing that horn!

Jan and Jenny just sat in an adjoining room listening to him play, thinking about songs they could sing together as a duet.

They finally decided to just grab a couple bowls and get some of that rocky road ice-cream from the freezer! As they ate the ice-cream, Jenny's mom reminded Jenny it was time for Jenny to do the dishes.

"I'll help!" Jan exclaimed, as if doing the dishes was a treat.

"Did you forget we don't have a dishwasher, because my mom refuses to let my dad buy one for her? She says the dishes get cleaner if you do them by hand."

"But she does have a dishwasher," Jan mused. "It's you!"

Jenny couldn't help but to laugh, in spite of herself.

"I have dishpan hands," she told Jan.

"Doesn't your sister take a turn doing the dishes?" Jan asked.

"Not a chance in a million!" Jenny told her. "She's the baby of the house."

"What about your brother?"

"He's a boy, Jan. Didn't you know dishes are a girl's job? And . . . I just happen to be the girl."

"What does your sister do?"

"Well . . . sometimes she does help out with the laundry," Jenny said, giving her younger sister a small amount of redemptive credit. "But other than that, she mainly has fun."

Jan said nothing in reply to that explanation, and after the two girls finished their rocky road ice-cream, and after they finished washing and drying and putting away the dishes, they headed off to Jenny's bedroom.

"I sure do love rocky road ice-cream," Jan mused as the two of them walked along.

Jenny nodded her head and said quietly under her breath, as if it was a secret, "Me too, Jan. I must confess that rocky road just happens to be my favorite!"

Soon it would be off to dreamland, after making plans for their very first delivery to the La Jolla Cove's Nursing Facility in the next few days. How exciting it was! And the girls truly hoped they would and could make a difference!

CHAPTER THIRTEEN

What A Difference A Day Makes!

Jan and Jenny were appalled when the President of The United States declared 99% of the Covid-19 cases caused no harm.

"Do you think he looked at the problem from a mathematical standpoint?" Jenny asked Jan, as they just stared at the living room television set, sipping their morning orange juice.

"I doubt it," Jan said, shaking her head. "It doesn't seem like the numbers would comply with that hypothesis."

"What's a hypothesis?" Christine asked, as she bounded into the room in her robe and slippers.

"Never mind," Jenny told her. "You wouldn't understand. Jan and I are discussing politics, and you wouldn't understand anything we are saying contextually."

"What does contextually mean?" Jenny's sister then asked.

"Never mind," Jenny repeated. "You wouldn't understand."

Jenny's sister then stomped her feet, insisting, "Yes, I would! Yes, I would! I'm no baby!"

"Fight nice, girls," Jenny's dad said as he entered the room, smelling fresh from his morning shower, dressed and ready to face the world.

"Where are you going?" Jenny asked, as her dad picked up his trumpet case from where it sat next to the piano.

"I'm off to my recording session," he replied, walking toward the front door, the television news blazing behind his voice in the background.

"Your recording session?" Jenny asked. "I thought that was in Los Angeles, and that it was called off during the Covid-19 crisis," she added, forgetting for the moment her dad had two recording contracts, one locally and one in Los Angeles.

"This is the local session, not the loss Angeles session," Jenny's dad said, as he stopped and turned to face the girls. "And we're being Covid-19 safe. We record one instrument at a time, while the previous recordings play . . . the ones recorded before I play. We record on different tracks; and then the recording engineer puts it all together at the end . . . well . . . something like that. And the sound engineer stays in a separate room behind a glass window all by himself, mixing the sound, with the final mix coming after everyone has recorded. I think I'm the final one on this track. Tomorrow we start another track . . . another piece of music."

"Sounds complex," Jan chimed in.

"It's work," Jan's dad told her. "And it puts the bread and butter on the table."

"Stay safe!" Jenny's mom shouted from the kitchen.

Jenny's dad smiled.

"I always do," he quipped, as he walked out the door. "I always do."

"And what do you girls have planned for today?" Jenny's mom asked, as she entered the room.

Jenny turned off the television set with the remote control, so her mother wouldn't be distracted.

"Do you think it would be possible for you to drive us down to the La Jolla Cove nursing home?" Jenny asked.

"Why in the world would you want to go there?" Jenny's mother asked.

"Because Jan and I have been sewing masks and making hand sanitizer out back in the camper . . ." Jenny began.

"I was wondering what you girls were doing out there," Jenny's mother said, interrupting Jenny.

Jenny took a deep breath.

"We would like to deliver the masks, latex gloves, and the hand sanitizer today; and we need a safe ride," Jenny said, in an attempt to flatter her mother.

"Is that all I am to you?" Jenny's mother asked. "Am I just a 'safe ride' to you?"

Well, I thought Jan and I could pack a car picnic; and we could all have a picnic in the car and watch the waves from Sunset Cliffs," Jenny added. "Well . . . that is . . ." Jenny paused for a moment, "that is . . . *after* we deliver the masks we sewed, along with the latex gloves, and the hand sanitizer we made."

"Not me! I don't want to go!" Jenny's sister shouted. "I want to play with my friends outside!"

Jenny's mom shook her head, and mouthed the word 'no', as she gave Christine one of her famous looks that said even more.

"I think a car picnic sounds like a great idea," she said. "And we will *all* go," she added giving Jenny's sister another one of her looks.

Jenny's bother would be no problem since there was food involved, so he was of no concern.

Little Christine finally relented. She even offered to help put the picnic lunch together.

As Jan and Jenny later filled the tan wicker picnic basket with sandwiches and single-sized bags of chips, and some apples, Jenny's mother exclaimed, "That picnic basket was probably the best purchase I ever made!"

Of course, before they left for the nursing home, Jan and Jenny had to do some clean-up, washing, drying and putting away the breakfast dishes; but that was okay, because Jan and Jenny were out to make a difference in the world! And, after all, that was *indeed* all that *really* mattered.

"You girls be safe doing this delivery . . ." Jenny's mother said in a not so sure voice, as they headed for the camper to retrieve all they had packed.

"We're just *dropping off* the masks, latex gloves, and hand sanitizer," Jenny explained. "And when we get there, all we have to do is put the masks (packed in the zip lock bags with the pairs of latex gloves) and the bottles of hand sanitizer at the front door, come back to the car, and then call and let the manager of the nursing home know the masks are there."

"And we can watch from where we're parked at the delivery curb out front to make sure they get them," Jan added. "It's simple, and it's safe. And it's all worked out!"

"When do we go to the picnic?" Jenny's bother, John, asked, as he entered the room.

"Right after we drop off everything," Jenny told him.

"Why can't we go swimming?" Christine whined. "I want to go swimming at the beach!"

"When we get home after the picnic, you can swim," Jenny's mom told her. "We *do* have a swimming pool, and you can swim there."

"That sounds like fun!" Jan exclaimed with delight!

"We can barbeque some hot dogs for dinner," Jenny's mom added. "And I have some homemade potato salad in the refrigerator . . . *and* we can even eat on paper plates!" she added with a smile.

Jenny sighed.

"It will be good to have a break from doing those dishes," she said, with a grin.

They all packed into the car, and before they even knew it, the five of them were at the nursing home!

As they pulled up to the delivery space in front of the nursing home, Jenny's mother asked, "Have I told you girls lately how proud I am of you?"

And those words made Jenny's day. It looked like they just might make a difference after all. (At least they got to eat on paper plates tonight!)

After that, it would be back to the drawing board, or should I say 'back to the sewing machine'?

They would have to resume their school internet studies on Monday, and Jan *did* have chores to do at home; but today was their day to make a difference; and the two girls hoped with all their hearts they could and would make a difference.

And so . . . they put the bags of the masks with the latex gloves and the five bottles of hand sanitizer (they had carefully placed in a sanitized, cardboard box) at the front door of the La Jolla Nursing Home, returned to the car, made the required phone call to the nursing home manager, and watched as the door opened, and as the box was removed from where it sat on the stoop. The manager gave the girls a big smile and a thumbs-up and mouthed the words, “Thank-you!”

Then, with tears in her eyes, the manager went back inside the nursing home; and she shut the door.

“I do think we made a difference!” Jenny exclaimed, and Jan agreed.

CHAPTER FOURTEEN

On To The picnic!

Jan and Jenny sat quietly in the back seat of Jenny's mom car, with Jenny's sister, Christine, sitting between them; and they drove to Sunset Cliffs. There were only a few cars there, so finding a parking space with a view of the Pacific Ocean below was a breeze!

"Why do we have to stop here?" Christine whined, as the car came to a stop and Jenny's mom set the parking brake. "Why are you doing that?" Christine asked.

"I'm setting the parking brake so we don't fall down the hill," Jenny's mother explained.

"When do we eat," Jenny's brother, John, asked from the front passenger side seat.

"If I still had my car seat I could see much better," Christine complained.

"Come sit on my lap, baby," Jenny's mother said, "and Jan and Jenny can pass out the delicious picnic lunch they packed for us."

"More room back here for us!" Jenny exclaimed, as she reached for the picnic basket sitting at her feet, and as Christine climbed over the front seat divider and took the offered place on Jenny's mother's lap.

"That's better!" Christine exclaimed, as she sat on her mother's lap. "I can see much better now!"

Jenny opened the picnic basket and passed the sandwiches one by one to Jan. Jan in turn passed the sandwiches forward to the front seat, all except for the two sandwiches meant for her and Jenny.

"I finally get to eat," John said, as he took it upon himself to distribute the three sandwiches passed up to him.

Then Jenny handed the still cold cans of soda to Jan, and the process was repeated. Finally, Jenny handed some paper napkins to Jan that Jan forwarded up to the front seat for distribution.

"This is fun!" Jenny's mother said, as she un-wrapped her sandwich.

Christine and John un-wrapped their sandwiches, as the cans of soda remained in the car cup holders where they had been paced after they were distributed.

"Yuck!" Christine complained. "I hate tuna fish! Why didn't you make me a peanut butter and jelly sandwich? I like those!"

"Since when have you hated tuna fish sandwiches?" Jenny's mother asked.

"Since Jenny made them," Christine whined, and as John gobbled up his sandwich.

"What's for dessert?" John asked, wiping his mouth on the paper napkin and opening up his can of soda.

"We are having Jan's world famous double chocolate chip brownies!" Jenny exclaimed, as she passed three bags of brownies directly up to the front seat.

Jan was glad she had made a double batch of brownies before she had headed up the hill to Jenny's house, because with what was left over from what she and Jenny had eaten prior to this, there was more than enough for the picnic!

"Look!" Jan suddenly shouted, as a California brown pelican perched itself on the hood of the car.

"Wow!" Jenny exclaimed. "How lucky could we get? I'd call that a bird's eye view!"

"Well," Jenny's brother, John, scoffed. "I'd say the bird has the bird's eye view, because he's a bird!"

The pelican moved toward the front window, and then it looked right inside the car.

"I guess he wants a better view," Jenny's mother surmised.

"Make it go away!" Christine screamed, as she climbed off her mother's lap and back over the front seat to her place in the back.

"Not on your life," Jenny's brother said. And then he asked, "Does anyone have a camera?"

"Our cell phones *all* have cameras!" Jenny exclaimed, as they all reached for their cell phones, quickly put them into camera mode, and began taking pictures of the bird with a bird's eye view of them.

And so . . . they all clicked away as the pelican took in an eyeful of them . . . . And Jenny simply could not believe her eyes!

"It's as though the pelican is posing for us!" Jenny said excitedly, as the pelican walked back and forth across the hood of the car, and they snapped away with their cell phones.

Of course, Christine was too young for a cell phone with a camera.

"This is so unfair," she complained.

"That's okay, baby," Jenny's mom said between the clicks of her cell phone camera. "When we get home, I'll fix you a peanut butter and jelly sandwich."

CHAPTER FIFTEEN

Quarantined!

Soon the picnic was over; at least it was over for the pelican, which with great aplomb flew from the hood of the car to join a flock of California brown pelicans as they flew above the water below the cliffs.

"Isn't that amazing?" Jenny asked, not expecting an answer.

"It sure is!" Jan exclaimed.

"Can we go home now?" Christine asked, ". . . so mom can make me a peanut butter and jelly sandwich?"

"If you aren't going to eat your tuna sandwich I'll eat it," Jenny's brother, John, offered.

"Too late," Christine told him. "It's already gone! I ate it! So, ha ha!"

John shrugged his shoulders, as Jenny's mom started the engine of the car; and they slowly pulled out of the parking space overlooking the cliffs, but not before Christine demanded she have a window seat for the trip back.

On the ride back from the Sunset Cliffs car picnic, Jan's cell phone rang. She saw it was her mom, so she answered the phone.

"Hi, Mom! What's up?" she asked.

Jan's mom had a worried tone in her voice.

"Hi, Sweetie," she said. "We have a slight problem."

"Really? It must be important, or you wouldn't call. What's wrong, Mom?"

Jan had a frightened look on her face, and so did Jenny after she saw Jan's expression.

"Your dad tested positive for Covid-19, so we are in lockdown here for the next two weeks, honey. I don't want you to worry; but can you ask Jenny's mom if you can stay at her house until then? We'll send some money for food and the extra necessities for your care, of course."

"Mom, let me call you back after we talk about this, because we're in the car now . . . okay?"

"Sure, honey. Now, don't be worried. Everything will be fine," Jan's mom reassuringly said, trying to convince both Jan and herself that everything would be okay.

"Ok. I love you. I'll call soon." Jan told her mother, trying to be brave.

Jan had a confused look on her face, as she glanced at Jenny and hung up the phone.

"Wow!" Jan exclaimed, "Did you hear that Jenny?" she asked, certain Jenny had overheard the conversation, since she was so close to her, now sitting right next to her in the backseat, with Christine now occupying the left side window seat, Jenny the right side window seat, and Jan now occupying the middle seat.

Jenny nodded and softly whispered, "Yes. I heard. I'm so sorry," as she looked up to the front at the rear view mirror, and saw her mom quickly look in the backseat.

"What's going on, girls?" she asked. "You look like the cats that just ate the little bird in the cage!" she stammered with concern, so much so that Jenny's mom almost missed the freeway turnoff that led to home!

"Oh, nothing much," both Jan and Jenny replied in unison, because (you see) they had an uncanny way of thinking alike.

Then they both started giggling in a vain attempt to hide the seriousness of what Jan had just been told.

"Mom!" Christine yelled. "I just know that Jan and Jenny are up to something!!! They always are. They should be punished!"

Just about then the car pulled into the driveway, and everybody bailed out fast. John went back to watching the television, commandeering his favorite spot, lying down just feet in front of it.

Christine ran into her room to put on her swimsuit, forgetting all about the peanut butter and jelly sandwich.

"The ocean waves made me want to swim!" she exclaimed, when her mother asked her why she put on her swimsuit instead of waiting for her sandwich.

"Go wait in the living room with your brother," Jenny's mom told Christine, who for once obliged without argument.

Meanwhile, Jan and Jenny had followed Jenny's mom into the kitchen, where they explained the current Covid-19 problem.

"Oh, my!" Jenny's mom exclaimed with great concern in her voice. "This pandemic is really getting bad! Thank goodness all our tests came back negative."

"They did?" Jenny asked.

"Oh . . . I guess I forgot to tell you with everything else going on . . ." she said apologetically. And then she quickly added, "I'm sure your dad won't have any problem with Jan staying here, but let's wait and ask him anyway, just so he thinks he was the one who made the final decision. Okay?" she asked with sly smile and a wink of her eye.

Then all three laughed together, because they knew women always got their way with men one way or another. And . . . after all, they did believe that someday women would ultimately rule the world!

(Jenny's dad called it 'using their feminine wiles'. And Jenny figured that was more than likely feminine wiles that gave Cleopatra her power over Anthony.)

After that, Jan and Jenny went into Jenny's room and put on their swimsuits. (Jan kept a swimsuit at Jenny's house, just for this reason!)

Jenny's mom prepared for the hot dog and potato salad barbeque.

A nice dip in the pool sounded like a great idea to Jan and Jenny! They could take some time to just relax and think about what steps the two of them could take next in order to unravel, and maybe to even *solve,* the mystery of Covid-19. Or perhaps it was even more than one mystery the two of them would have to unravel and solve! Only the future would tell; and Jenny was figuring the answers would be found right there on their cell phones and computers.

"It's a good thing you brought your laptop in that bulging backpack of yours," Jenny told Jan. "Now we can work on two levels!"

"Maybe we can even work on more levels than that!" Jan replied confidently. "We are very good at multi-tasking, after all."

And as to that, Jenny agreed; and the two of them grabbed their towels from the linen cupboard in the hall, and headed toward the backyard pool!

CHAPTER SIXTEEN

The Swim!

"Do you girls mind watching Christine while you're in the pool? I'll be out there soon!" Jenny's mom yelled after the two girls as they headed toward the backyard pool, towels in hand, Christine rushing to catch up with them.

"No problem!" The girls yelled back, once again in unison.

Giggling, the girls walked through the kitchen, and then the laundry room, and then right out the back door.

"We have to be careful not to let the dog out," Jenny said, as she slowly lifted the latch on the back yard redwood fence gate.

"Okay," Jan told her, as they walked through the open gate.

"You care more about that old dog than you care about me," Christine said, as Jenny bent over to greet her dog.

Jenny ignored Christine, as Jan said, "I sure do miss my dog, Sasha."

"I know," Jenny said softly, as she closed the gate behind them, "but look how happy Soxy is to see you!"

"I know. But I still miss my little Sasha."

"You'll be home before you know it, Jan," Jenny told her, as Christine headed for the pool.

"Get one of those lifesaver rings from the box by the pool!" Jenny shouted to her sister, watching happily, as Christine complied.

And then, before the girls knew it, Jenny's dad was there, clad in his swimming trunks, setting up the old record player to play some vintage jazz classics pressed in vinyl that he still happened to have!

"You know, those old records are probably worth a small fortune," Jan quipped.

"Well, I think they mean more than just money to my dad," Jenny told her, as her dad dove into the swimming pool from the side of the deep end. "You know, he *always* tells me to listen to those records," she added. "He says if I want to learn how to sing, I need to listen."

"Do you do that, Jenny?"

"Of course, I do, Jan! Everyone does what my dad says if they know what is good for them."

"What do you mean?" Jan asked.

"Well, he has this knowing thing. He knows stuff before it happens."

"Like what, Jenny?"

"Well . . ." Jenny told her, hesitating; "he knew about this pandemic. He knew it was coming."

Jan's eyes grew wide.

"He just started talking about the great pandemic of 1918, and then he said we should be ready for another one."

"That's spooky, Jenny."

"I guess so, Jan; but he also said someday I would be just like him and that I would know things."

"Do you believe that, Jenny? Do you really believe that?"

"I do, Jan. I believe it. Do you want to know why?"

"Why, Jenny?"

"Well, I'm already having these strange dreams, Jan. And those dreams are scary. I see my father dying. And I have the dream all the time."

"Do you think he will die in the pandemic?"

"No. He won't die yet. But he will be young. And my mom will marry again. However, I think I will be grown up then. I think I will even be married."

"That's really weird, Jenny."

"It is weird, Jan; so don't tell anyone I told you about it. Okay? Because people will think I'm crazy."

"Are you a witch, Jenny?"

"No. I'm not a witch, Jan. I just know stuff, like my dad. And I don't know why I know what I know."

"Will my mom and dad and sister die of Covid-19, Jenny?"

"I don't see that happening, Jan. But I do know that more people will die before this is over; and not only old people will die like they say."

Jenny's dad popped his head up from swimming underwater.

"Hey! You girls are supposed to be having some fun," he said, as Christine happily bobbed around in her lifesaver ring!

Suddenly, John dashed through the gate, letting it literally slam behind him.

"Don't run on the wet deck!" Jenny's mom yelled as she opened the slammed gate and appeared with a tray of barbeque fixings.

Jenny's bother, John, ignored her and ran across the wet deck to the pool deck's deep end.

"Cannonball!" he yelled as he took the cannonball position and splashed into the water.

"That boy just never listens," Jenny's mom said, as Jenny's father got out of the pool to help Jenny's mom with the barbeque tray.

As Jenny's dad took the condiments from Jenny's mom, he said, "We all need to make fun while the sun shines!"

And as the music played, a sunset filled the sky.

"Isn't it lovely, Jenny?" Jan asked.

And it was all very lovely as the music played, and as they made fun happen as the sun went down.

"Life is what you make of it," Jenny's dad said, as he got out of the pool at the shallow end, wrapped a dry towel around his waist that he had earlier placed on the picnic table bench, and turned on the gas barbecue.

Jenny watched her father place the hotdogs on the gas grill, knowing that what her father said was always true; and this was because her father was *never* wrong. And Jenny also knew that things in the world were not quite right, right now. And she knew that she and Jan had to do something about it before it was too late. And this is how the two of them became internet detectives!

CHAPTER SEVENTEEN

Back to The Command Center!

After the swim and fun barbecue, Jan and Jenny headed back to the camper/Command Center to continue with their work, making masks and searching the internet for any clues they could discover about the Covid-19 pandemic that might lead them to discovering who was really behind this whole catastrophe, and how they could once and for all solve the Covid-19 mystery.

But they really didn't think they would or could actually discover who or what was behind Covid-19, and they figured that if they could help just one person, this might be all they could do.

On their walk to the camper, Jan was thinking about what Jenny told her about "knowing" things before they happened; and it reminded her of a movie called 'The 'Shining', where a little boy had that same unique ability.

"Jenny," Jan asked, "have you ever seen the movie or read the book by Stephen King called, 'The Shining'?"

Jenny gasped and replied, "Are you kidding? That guy is scary! His books scare me to death. No way will I read his stuff. You're the one who likes horror movies, not me!"

Jan laughed; and then she said, "Well, the reason I asked is because one of the characters in the book had that knowing thing you and your dad have. It's called 'shining'. I thought that was cool. Not very many people can do that. I think it's like being clairvoyant, isn't it?"

"I think that's another word for it, or it's similar anyway. I can't really explain it. But it's not always fun to know things ahead of time, let me tell you," Jenny replied. "And I really have no control about what I will know. It just comes to me, and it seems rather random. My dad says someday I will be able to look at a person and know everything about them, but I'm not sure that would be a good thing. It's kind of scary knowing things before they happen. All you do is know things. But you can't change anything, because what will be will be. So I really don't understand the purpose of it."

Jan just shrugged her shoulders, because she thought it was awesome to have that ability. It might even come in handy, she thought, in solving their current pandemic case! Maybe it wouldn't, if it was true they couldn't change the future; but just perhaps . . . maybe some 'knowing' wouldn't hurt. (However, knowing how

Jenny felt about it, Jan decided she would keep that thought to herself for now, since Jenny was so sensitive and touchy about the subject.

The two girls arrived at the camper and went inside, ready to get to work. Swimsuits now dry, they left them on, set the mask making materials aside for the moment, and went straight to their laptops to start searching for information on the Covid-19 virus. They'd already used up all of the ingredients for making hand sanitizer, keeping just enough for themselves and Jenny's family. (Jan had made some at her house, and had left it there for *her* family.)

Jan was the first one to find something new on the computer.

"Look, Jenny!" she exclaimed with excitement, "our nursing home in La Jolla (the one we gifted the masks, latex gloves and hand sanitizer) was just gifted (from an anonymous donor) fifty iPads for the residents, so that they can safely communicate with their loved ones and friends! Now we're getting somewhere! We can start writing them, and maybe we can learn some more information from them about what's going on with this virus. You know, senior nursing facilities have had one of the highest rates of mortality from the Covid-19 virus so far. I think it's terrible! They deserve much better care than most of them are apparently receiving, don't you think?"

Jenny nodded her head in agreement, as she scrolled down her computer screen looking through the newest posted numbers of Covid-19 cases and deaths in California.

Shaking her head in disbelief at what she was reading, she suddenly looked straight at Jan and said in disgust, "We have got to do something about this pronto, Jan! This is no way for any of us to be living our lives, all cooped up inside our homes, and not knowing what to believe anymore!"

Jan and Jenny to the rescue!" Jan shouted.

"And on that note let's have a snack!" Jenny exclaimed.

And . . . Jan headed straight for the mini-fridge.

"A girl after my own heart," Jenny laughed.

So snack time it was!

CHAPTER EIGHTEEN

The Computer Search Begins Again!

"We need to know more about this stuff," Jenny said, as she scoured the internet. There are so many conflicting messages out there!"

"I'll say," Jan mumbled, somewhat distracted.

"What's wrong, Jan?" Jenny asked.

"Is that the knowing thing talking?" Jan grimaced.

"No. It's the look on your face, Jan. I can tell that you're worried," Jenny told her. "So, please tell me what's bothering you."

"Everything!" Jan suddenly shouted. "My dad tested positive for Covid-19, and the entire world is about to end!"

There was a knock at the camper door.

"Who is it?" Jenny shouted as she turned to look in the direction of the camper door.

"It's your dad!" came the reply.

Jenny got up and went to the door and opened it.

"What's up?" she asked.

"I was just talking to Jan's parents, and her dad's Covid-19 test was a false positive."

"They made a mistake?" Jan asked, somewhat timidly, as she rose to her feet.

"Yes," Jenny's father told her. "But . . ."

"There's a 'but'?" Jan asked.

"Yes," Jenny's father told her, lowering his eyes. "Even though his test was a false positive, your family still has to quarantine for the next fourteen days; because another guy in your dad's unit *did* actually test positive for Covid-19."

"Can I stay here, then?" Jan asked.

"Of course you can stay here, Jan. You don't even have to ask. You're just like a member of our family!"

I guess that makes us sisters, Jan." Jenny laughed.

"Singing sisters!" Jan exclaimed, all worry now fading from her face.

"Hey, you two should call yourselves 'The Singing Sisters' when you perform!" Jenny's dad told them.

"That's a great idea!" the girls shouted excitedly in unison.

"And speaking of that, I have your first Covid-19 venue," Jenny's father added.

"Where?" Jenny asked, somewhat bewildered.

"It's a virtual venue," Jenny's dad explained. "And we can do it together with some of my musician friends on a multi-split screen."

Jan and Jenny beamed.

"I'll fill you in later, when the plans are finalized," Jenny's father told them. "In the meantime, you can return to making those masks!"

Jenny could see Jan was feeling much better after hearing the news that her father had a false positive. Nothing more was said on the subject, although Jenny could see Jan was visibly relieved.

Jan turned on the television set. And as the two of them listened for updates on Covid-19, they got the news that a twenty year old, previously healthy, young man had died from the virus. As they listened and watched, they discovered the reason why the young man had died! He went to a Covid-19 party and purposely exposed himself to someone who had tested positive for the virus and was asymptomatic, thinking he wouldn't get the virus, and if he got the virus, he would have only a mild case of Covid-19; and then he would become immune to it.

"They said only the old people and people with underlying conditions would die of this thing!" Jan exclaimed in disbelief.

Jenny continued to scour the internet as the television blazed on . . . not far from where the two girls sat.

"Apparently, believing he could't *or* wouldn't get Covid-19, *and* if he did get it, it wouldn't be serious, and then he'd be immune, was *completely* wrong," Jenny mumbled in astonishment.

"It's a sad way to learn a hard lesson, Jenny . . . a sad way indeed!"

"And now here you go," Jenny replied, looking up from her laptop, "I just found *another* Covid-19 party! It's right here on the internet! And . . . it's not far from here! And it's a bunch of kids, not too much older than *we are* that are having the party!"

"Are those kids crazy?" Jan asked. And then she added, "What can we do?"

"Well, we are certainly *not* going to that party!" Jenny told her.

"Do you think the authorities know about it, Jenny?"

"Well, Jan, if they don't know about it now, they will soon find out about it," Jenny said, as she picked up her cell phone and began to dial 911.

"What's the rush?" Jan asked.

"It's set for tonight," Jenny told her. "It's going to happen in just a few hours." she added.

Jenny put her mobile device on speaker, so Jan could hear.

"911," came the female voice on the other side of the call. "Please state the nature of your emergency."

Jenny explained what she had found on the internet, and gave the 911 operator the address where the party was to be held.

"We'll send officers over there right away," the 911 operator told her. "And thank you for calling."

With those words, the conversation with the 911 operator ended.

"Do you think that internet posting was a hoax?" Jan asked.

"I don't think so," Jenny replied.

"It's hard to believe *anyone* would be so stupid that they would host a Covid-19 party, right after the news announced a twenty year old, previously healthy, young man had died because of one of those parties."

"Maybe the host was just misinformed, Jan."

"Or maybe those kids don't watch the news like we do, Jenny"

"Somebody has to do something!" Jan added imploringly.

"We can only do what we can do," Jenny told her. "And we just need to work harder."

"Harder?" Jan asked.

"My mom always says, 'Hard work never hurt anyone.' And I suppose you and I are about to find out if that's true," Jenny told her, to which Jan whole heartedly agreed!

CHAPTER NINETEEN

Time To Ask The Hufflefingers

There are so many conflicting messages out there!" Jan exclaimed, as she began wracking her brain, trying to figure out how the Covid-19 pandemic started.

Jenny was more interested in locating violators of the Governor's rules about social distancing and in making personal protective equipment for people to wear to keep everyone safer from *getting* Covid-19.

They *both* agreed that it was quite apparent with the rising number of cases and deaths in California alone, that this disease wasn't going away anytime soon. Kids weren't even going to be allowed to return to school for the fall semester! And Jan, especially, was perplexed and frustrated; because *she* wanted to save the world from this terrible pandemic! And Jenny was anxious to slow the surge by providing masks and reporting Covid-19 parties to the authorities wherever she could find them to save humanity. These were big shoes for two young girls to fill, for sure. But they felt in their hearts that they were up to the tasks!

Jan began thinking about the other cases they had solved in the past. They had really made progress with those cases when they contacted their retired CIA friends, Mr. and Mrs. Hufflefinger.

"That's it! We should contact the Hufflefingers via Skype!" Jan thought exuberantly to herself. "They'll know what to do!"

It had been some time since the two girls had spoken with the Hufflefingers, but that was mostly due to the pandemic and all the restrictions being imposed on the human race! They couldn't even visit their neighborhood friends, so a trip to the Hufflefingers to visit them (and their chickens, carrier pigeons, and ducks) was out of the question.

"Yes! That just might be the solution!" Jan surmised, now convinced she only had to convince Jenny, who was now busily sewing masks at the sewing station they'd set up in the camper.

"Oh, Jenny," Jan sheepishly began, "I think I have a brilliant idea."

Jenny looked up from her sewing and asked, "And what might that be? I know that tone of voice, and you happen to have that tell-tale sheepish grin on your face. So . . . okay . . . spit it out, Jan!"

Jan smiled. Jenny knew her all too well.

"What do you think about Skyping the Hufflefingers for their sage advice?" she began. "They might have some connections who can help us get on the correct track, so that we can discover some answers to all the unknown questions we have about what's actually going on with Covid-19. I mean . . . they *are* ex-CIA secret agents. We need all the help we can get!"

"Well . . . well," Jenny replied; and then . . . after she thought for a moment, she suddenly exclaimed, "That is a great idea! Why didn't I think of that? Let's do it! And they have lots of contacts! That's for sure! I'm excited to hear from them too! It's been quite a while."

It certainly appeared that Jan didn't have to convince Jenny after all!

Jan smiled and squealed from excitement.

"I'm so glad you agree! I think I still have their computer contact information in the old backpack I brought with me for the sleepover. I'll check right now!"

"How did you know you'd be sleeping over?" Jenny asked, remembering the bulging, heavy backpack Jan carried up the hill.

"It always helps to be prepared!" Jan laughed, as she headed for her backpack. "I didn't exactly bring enough for two weeks, but I figure I can just wash and dry my clothes with yours. After all, we aren't exactly going much of anywhere; *and* we are very unlikely to run into any cute boys, or even any of our classmates," Jan mumbled almost to herself, as Jenny went back to frantically sewing more masks, and as Jan rummaged through her now in hand backpack.

"I found it!" Jan shouted with relief, a bit of sweat dripping from her forehead from exerting nearly all her energy searching through the still overly stuffed backpack for the Hufflefinger contact information.

"That's terrific!" Jenny told Jan. "Now, before we Skype the Hufflefingers, please get over here and help me make some more masks. Okay? That's one thing that will always be needed until a cure is found."

"Sure thing, Commander!" Jan replied. "It's getting a little late in the day to contact them now, anyway. We can Skype them bright and early tomorrow! I'm so excited! Yay!" Jan shouted.

Jenny echoed Jan's "Yay!" as she continued sewing masks, and said, "Now get over here and help me! We have a ton of work to do!"

And so for the moment, they put all of their concentration back into making the much needed facial masks for those in need, knowing in their hearts that tomorrow was going to (hopefully) be a great day!

CHAPTER TWENTY

Sew & Reap

Jan and Jenny sewed and cut, and cut and sewed, and between all of that, they took some time to research on the web. Finally, they decided it was time to sleep, or rather Jenny's mom decided it was time for them to get some sleep.

A knock came at the camper door and Jenny's mom's voice rang out, "I know you two are out to save the world again!" Jenny's mom shouted, as Jan hopped over to the door, dodging the scraps of fabric strewn about on the camper floor. "But I *do think* it is now time for you two to hit the hay."

"Five more minutes?" Jenny begged, as Jan motioned Jenny's mom to enter.

"I'll give you ten more minutes, and I'll add an extra five minutes if you two clean up this floor," she said, as Jenny continued to sew another mask.

"You've got a deal," Jenny said, without looking up from the task at hand. "But can we sleep out here tonight?"

"You can sleep out here," Jenny's mother told them, "if I see the lights out in exactly fifteen minutes, *and* if you *promise* to pick up the mess you made in here."

"We promise!" Jan told her, as she began picking up the scraps of material, thread, and other sewing debris off of the floor, putting all of it into the nearby trashcan, an armful at a time.

Jenny's mother shook her head.

"You girls are working *way* too hard," she told them, as she turned and reopened the camper door and began to walk down the outside camper stairs. Without looking back, she shouted, "Now I'm counting on your promise! And I still say you two are working way too hard!" she added, as the camper door shut behind her.

As Jenny continued to sew, she shouted back, "But you told me no one ever died of hard work, Mom! And that Hard work never hurt anyone!"

As Jenny's mother walked toward the back door of the house she mumbled to herself, "Well . . . I *did* say that, but if anybody *could* die from hard work, it would be those two girls . . . and I did mean that to apply to doing the *dishes* when I said it . . . but I guess somebody *does* have to save the world . . . I just wish that it didn't have to be those two! It's driving me crazy!"

The girls did as they were told, and turned off the lights according to the pre-set agreement. They changed into their pajamas and climbed into the bunks in the back of the camper, leaving only the television running on the "News All Nite' channel, just to make sure they wouldn't miss out on anything. They figured a running television wasn't a light, and that it would serve them well as not only a point of information, but it would also serve them as a night light in case they had to use the camper toilet.

"We sewed another fifty masks tonight," Jenny said, with a somewhat tired sigh, as she climbed up into the top bunk, placed her head on the pillow, and pulled up the top sheet and blanket to cover her.

"That many?" Jan asked, rather surprised at the number, and having already tucked herself into bed, as she had been the first to claim and to crawl under the covers of the bottom bunk.

"Yup!" Jenny proudly replied. "I think we're getting faster and better at this sewing thing!"

"Well . . . you know what your mother always says . . . 'You only reap what you sew . . ."

"My mother says a lot of things, Jan. And I think she meant the other kind of sow!"

"It's really all the same thing, Jenny . . . don't ya think?"

"I guess so . . ." Jenny replied with a yawn; and then before they knew it, the two girls fell fast asleep.

"In the morning we'll Skype the Hufflefingers," Jan said, as she drifted off into a deep, deep sleep.

The 'News All Nite' channel continued to blare, as it tried to sneak its way into their dreams. And only one thing was certain, these two girls were simply out to save the world; and no matter what may come their way, they were very, very determined that this was *exactly* what they were going to do!

CHAPTER TWENTY-ONE

Meet Mrs. Chen

The sun was rising, and its glare shone through the camper window right into Jan's closed, sleeping eyes . . . suddenly waking her from her slumber.

"Hey, Jenny, what time is it anyway? The sun woke me up!"

Jenny mumbled back, "Well, it didn't wake me up! Put your head under the covers, and go back to sleep, Jan! It's barely 6:00 AM!"

Jan rolled out of her bunk and turned off the TV. (That thing blaring would *never* let her go back to sleep!) Then she jumped back into bed, pulled the covers up over her head; and it wasn't too long before she was back asleep.

(Both girls *did* love their beauty sleep!)

After a couple of hours in deep sleep, Jan started having a Covid-19 nightmare that caused her to abruptly sit straight up in bed!

And to make matters worse, she ended up hitting the top of her head on Jenny's overhead bunk, jostling Jenny's bunk, waking up Jenny!

"Ouch," Jan yelled. "That hurt!"

"Are you ok, Jan," Jenny asked, yawning and rubbing her eyes.

"I just had a horrible Covid-19 nightmare! The hospitals were all at maximum capacity, all the respirators and the ventilators were in use; and they had huge moving vans at the back of the hospitals where they were putting all the dead bodies! It was horrible!"

Jan started crying.

"Well, I hate to tell you this, but that's no nightmare, Jan. It's reality! I just heard on the news last night that over twenty-four of the states here in our country are dealing with that *very* problem! And I'm sure it's even worse in other countries that aren't as lucky as we are to have the medical service and care we have here in the United States that we Americans just take for granted."

Jan sobbed, and then paused to blow her nose on a tissue she took from the box of tissues that sat on the floor next to the bottom bunk where she now sat upright.

"You're completely right, Jenny," she said, as she gained her composure. "This disease is totally out of control! Let's have breakfast and Skype the Hufflefingers immediately. I really hope they are up this early . . . though . . . they're pretty old, ya know."

"How do pancakes sound to you?" Jenny asked, momentarily changing the subject. "I feel like cooking!" Jenny said, as she jumped down from the top bunk, did ten quick jumping jacks, brushed her hair, put on her slippers and robe and dashed out the camper door to the house, not even waiting for Jan's response.

Jan just shook her head, got herself together, and followed Jenny inside the house to the kitchen.

Jan had long ago discovered that when Jenny had her mind set on doing something, it was best to just get out of the way and let her do her thing. And since Jan was also pretty spontaneous, just like Jenny, it didn't bother her at all.

Jan brought her laptop with her to the kitchen, along with the Hufflefinger contact information for their Skype session. And while Jenny cooked, Jan Skyped!

They were the only two in the house at the moment. Jenny's mom, dad, John and Christine had taken a morning walk around the neighborhood, wearing the protective face masks Jan and Jenny had sewn for them, right after Jenny's dad had taken himself, Christine and John for their Covid-19 tests. Walking was a sort of morning ritual now. Exercise kept their anxiety down to a minimum.

Luckily for them, Jenny's dad was able to get nearly instant results of their Covid-19 tests at the doctor's office, because the doctor hurried them along and read the tests himself; and Jenny's dad, sister and brother were all negative, just like Jan and Jenny and

Jenny's mom! And as the rest of the family walked on their morning walk, Jenny's dad called her from his cell phone (to her cell phone) to give the girls the good news! Jan and Jenny were delighted!

Meanwhile, as the rest of the family continued their morning walk, Jan manned the computer; and Jenny manned the kitchen stove!

"Ok, Jenny . . . here goes! Keep your fingers crossed!" Jan exclaimed, as Jenny flipped the first pan of pancakes.

And . . . within a couple of minutes on the keyboard, Jan had contacted The Hufflefingers.

First, Jan spoke. She voiced all of the usual pleasantries when Mr. Hufflefinger appeared on screen, and she told him she and Jenny were checking on them to see how they were doing during the pandemic. Both girls were pleased to find that they were doing well. Jenny turned off the stove and brought the pancakes to the table, and stood behind Jan, waving at Mr. Hufflefinger, who happily waved back.

"It's so good to see you two girls again!" Mr. Hufflefinger exclaimed delightedly, as he called his wife to come over and join in the conversation.

"It's Jan and Jenny, honey! Say 'Hi'," he directed.

Mrs. Hufflefinger placed her hands on her husband's shoulders and leaned toward the screen to speak.

"Well, howdy doo, girls! You both look wonderful! What have you been up to these days? It's surprising to see you together with the virus going on now."

Both Jan and Jenny started to talk at the same time. And then they looked at each other and laughed.

So did the Hufflefingers.

Jenny motioned to Jan and gave her the floor.

"Well, it's a long story," Jan began, "but I'll try and make it short. My family is in quarantine for two weeks, because my dad was exposed to the virus at work. I had been staying with Jenny for a couple of days, and we got tested. Jenny and I and Jenny's Mom had negative tests, and the rest of her family had their Covid-19 tests early this morning. (Jenny's dad took her sister and brother for testing and they were all negative) so I'm staying here for the next two weeks. We've been making masks for senior nursing homes mainly, but we wanted to do more! We thought you might be able to lead us in the right direction and give us some ideas about what we could do to help out. So far, we've been working with the La Jolla Nursing Home on Cove Avenue. They've been very nice to us."

Mr. Hufflefinger rubbed the bottom of his chin with the fingers of his right hand, as if he was trying to think; and then Mrs. Hufflefinger spoke.

"Let me sit down, honey," she said, "and talk to them and tell them about Mrs. Chen."

"Oh, that's a terrific idea, dear," Mr. Hufflefinger told her, as he got up from his chair and gently helped his wife to sit in his place.

"Well, girls, it just so happens we have a very dear friend residing at that very same nursing home. She is so dear to us, and she's a very sweet Chinese lady we used to work with back in the day. She developed a case of early onset dementia, and her son, who is a renowned chemist here in San Diego, had to place her in their care about a year ago. She has many moments of clarity. I feel like you would be good for her, and that she would love to have you as either pen pals or Zoom friends, or one of those many ways people communicate by computer these days. The residents there are quite lonely without family visitation, and they haven't been able to see family since the virus came upon us. She probably has friends there who would love to have outsiders contact them for conversation. We could give you her email, and you could contact her! She's a very interesting woman with an even more interesting past!"

Jenny nodded her head in agreement, and Jan excitedly exclaimed, "That would be great! And we'll keep in contact with you as well, if you would like that. We can update you on her condition."

"Why, of course, Jan. We wouldn't have it any other way!" Mrs. Hufflefinger replied, smiling. "It was good talking with you. Keep us updated. Don't forget now!"

"Don't worry about that!" Jenny said, peeking down over Jan's shoulder at the computer screen. "You know us! We love to get involved!"

Both Mr. and Mrs. Hufflefinger laughed, remembering all their past encounters. Jan jotted down Mrs. Chen's email address, and they waved good-bye. The Skype session was finished. And it appeared to be a success!

"Well," Jan sheepishly asked, "How do you feel about cold pancakes, Jenny?"

"What do you think microwave ovens are for?" Jenny asked, grabbing the plate of pancakes to heat them in the microwave.

"Just don't microwave them for too long," Jan warned. "I don't like cardboard pancakes!"

Laughter ensued, and they finally got to eat their pancakes. And just as they were finishing up, Jenny's family arrived home.

"Well," Jan said, as she grabbed her laptop from off the table, "I'd say it's time for us to go and make a new friend!"

Jenny put their eating utensils and plates into the empty kitchen sink; and out the backdoor they went, as the rest of Jenny's family entered through the front door.

"I'll come back and do the dishes later!" Jenny shouted as she and Jenny left the house and headed back to Command Central. "And by the way," Jenny added, still shouting and on the move, "I left pancake batter in the fridge, and there's enough for everyone!"

"Yummy!" Christine exclaimed. "I love pancakes!"

"Who doesn't love pancakes?"Jenny's brother, John, added.

"Thank-you!" Jenny's mother shouted back as the back door slammed behind the two girls.

"Jenny makes good pancakes," Christine said, looking up at her mother.

"Yes, she does," Jenny's mother told her. "And don't you forget to thank her for all the nice things she does."

:

CHAPTER TWENTY-TWO

Everything Happens For A Reason

Once they'd returned to Command Central, Jan and Jenny, immediately sat themselves down and got to work.

"I'll sew, and you work on that email, Jan," Jenny directed.

"Aye! Aye!" Jan laughed.

The sun was finished rising, and now it was getting rather hot in the camper.

Jenny turned on a nearby fan that sat on a bookcase under the camper window closest to them.

"It's going to be a hot day," Jenny said.

"Ya think?" Jan quipped, but not complaining.

Jenny began to sew; and Jan emailed Mrs. Chen a kind introduction, telling her Mr. and Mrs. Hufflefinger suggested she and Jenny could be Skype friends with her, if she was so inclined.

And almost as soon as Jan hit the send button, there was a reply.

"Oh, no," Jan mumbled to herself, loud enough for Jenny to hear. "I guess I came on too strong and she thinks we're con artists or spammers or something. That was way too quick an answer," Jan added as she opened the incoming email.

Jenny stopped sewing, as Jan let out a happy shriek!

"She wants to Skype with us, Jenny! She wants to Skype right now!"

Before the two girls knew it, there they were . . . face to face, or rather computer to computer . . . talking to Mrs. Chen.

"I am so pleased you emailed me," Mrs. Chen began. "And I'm even more pleased that I am having a good day today," she added.

Jan and Jenny quickly introduced themselves.

"There is something I need to get off my chest," Mrs. Chen told them. "So please let me tell you, so that you can convey this to my dear friends, the Hufflefingers. You see, I worked undercover with them long ago; and I know they will know what to do about this."

"About what?" Jan asked. "Please tell us. We want to help with whatever it is," she added.

Jenny's eyes widened. This thing was going to be big. She just knew it.

"My dear son told me something. I was supposed to tell the Hufflefingers. He also was working undercover, you see. I was the only one he could go to with this information. He said it was too dangerous to go anywhere else, because he would blow his cover."

Jenny felt like her heart was rising into her throat and wondered about what this could be.

And Jan, who was usually the calmer of the two, wrote on a piece of paper in front of her the words, "Should we be scared?"

Gaining her composure, Jenny said, "Okay. Go ahead and tell us. We will do our best to help in whatever way we possibly can."

Then Mrs. Chen began her tale, it was something the girls never expected. Either what she was saying was true, or this woman was completely out of her mind! Either way, the girls would keep their promise; and they would forward the message about what Mrs. Chen had told them to the Hufflefingers.

When Mrs. Chen finished her story, she thanked the girls for listening and then added, "The thing about this information is that even though it comes from a good source, who will ever believe an old woman with early onset dementia?"

"Maybe that's why your son told you about it," Jenny said.

"He thought it would be safe with you; and you would know who to tell," Jan added.

"I tried telling the doctors, and they only increased my medication . . . so much so, that I couldn't function well, much less think. So I got a message out to the Hufflefingers to send me someone I could tell this to, so I could get the burden off of my shoulders."

"What happened to your son?" Jenny asked, fearing the answer.

"They killed him," Mrs. Chen said, with tears running down her face. "My precious son is dead. They gave him the virus. He was patient zero."

CHAPTER TWENTY-THREE

Huge Stuff!

After the Skype connection was discontinued, Jan and Jenny sat silently for a minute, contemplating what they had just heard.

"We need to contact the Hufflefingers this very minute!!" Jenny exclaimed.

I think I'm getting scared, Jenny . . . I think I'm really afraid this time. Do you think our government, or the Chinese government, will be tracking us now?"

"Look, Jan," Jenny began, "the Hufflefingers are ex-CIA. They'll know what to do with this. So let's get in touch with them right now!"

"Do you think the link will be safe, Jenny?"

"No one even knows we exist in this thing. All we did was to continue something we started, helping people in a nursing home. There's no need for anyone to suspect us of knowing anything."

"We haven't exactly done anything, anyway, not really," Jan mumbled back. "We only talked to a senile old lady."

"That's our story. And if anyone asks, we're sticking to it. All we've done is talk to an old lady and our friends, Mr. and Mrs. Hufflefinger. Besides, they'll know what to do about this, Jan. They've always helped us when we needed help in the past. And we're just a couple of kids! What can a couple of kids do anyway? No one would ever believe what we were told!"

With that said, Jan agreed the two of them should get the Hufflefingers up on the computer screen; and so they did just that!

Jenny's heart was pounding.

"We talked to Mrs. Chen," Jenny began, after the pleasantries of the introduction were completed. "And she told us something about her son and his company."

Then Jenny began the story, ending with the fact Mrs. Chen told them her son was patient zero.

The Hufflefingers were not surprised.

"We're sorry to put you two sweet girls in that position," Mr. Hufflefinger said. "But we needed to confirm the story."

"I don't understand," Jenny interjected.

"We needed to find out if this was simply a false memory or a delusion brought on by the drugs she was taking," Mr. Hufflefinger told the girls, who were both sitting in front of the computer screen wide-eyed.

"But she told us she wanted us to tell you," Jan protested.

"I don't think that she remembers talking to you at all," Jenny added.

"She probably doesn't remember talking to us, the sweet dear," Mrs. Hufflefinger said, as she looked over Mr. Hufflefinger's shoulders into their computer screen.

"Sadly, it is one of the many affects of her early onset dementia," Mr. Hufflefinger further explained. "Sometimes she remembers things, and sometimes she just forgets. This is why we wanted you girls to make a connection. It seems she remembers what her son told her. And she remembers he died, and how he ended up dying."

"But you didn't tell us he was dead," Jan said. "Why didn't you tell us that?"

"We didn't want to taint the evidence of the statement," Mr. Hufflefinger told the girls. "We had to make sure what she told you was consistent with what she told us."

"How do you prove that?" Jenny asked.

"Well . . ." Mr. Hufflefinger confessed, "we bugged Mrs. Chen's link, or rather we have an ongoing hack into her feed."

Suddenly, attorney Wright's voice could be heard saying something in the background.

"Is that who I think it is?" Jenny asked. "Is that our old friend, attorney Wright?"

"It's me!" Attorney Wright announced, as she peered over Mr. Hufflefinger's other shoulder. "And I want to thank you girls for all your help. Now I can prove our case."

Jan and Jenny shook their heads in amazement. This looked like a possible treason against the American people! And this wasn't even considering that a world-wide pandemic had been unleashed.

"So this is true? What we were told is true?" Jan asked sheepishly.

"No one can say for sure, but it *does* appear so."

"You mean people would let a virus out to make a profit on a vaccine?"

"I think things got out of hand," attorney Wright began. "I think they thought they had a vaccine; but when push came to shove (so to speak) the vaccine wasn't fully developed. It turned out to be unsafe in its present state. I think what they wanted was government funding."

"Will they get it?" Jenny asked. "Will they get government funding to finish their vaccine development?"

"I don't think so. But I think the fault of this doesn't lie with the researchers. It only lies at the top, and we'll do our best to get the guys at the top; and then . . . hopefully the researchers will work with the World Health Organization and others and develop a vaccine."

"Is Mrs. Chen going to be safe?" Jan asked. "She seemed too sweet."

"She was a great undercover agent in her day; and so was her son up until the time he died, so we'll take good care of her," attorney Wright explained,

"But how?" Jan asked, skeptically.

"We're going to put her in protective care, and we'll assign a private nurse to care for her. She'll have nothing but the best! She will want for nothing!" Ms. Wright told them.

"But she won't have her son," Jan said sadly.

"When will this happen?" Jenny asked.

"It's happening as we speak," attorney Wright told the girls.

"Right now?"Jenny asked.

"Right now!" attorney Wright said with enthusiasm.

The connection was soon closed, but Jan and Jenny were still frightened by all they had heard and by what they now knew. They promised to keep what they had been told and learned in strictest confidence and attorney Wright and the Hufflefingers *knew* Jan and Jenny could be trusted with the information they had heard and had been given.

CHAPTER TWENTY-FOUR

A New Beginning

They knew it was going to be a new beginning for Mrs. Chen, as they packed her bags and all her belongings at the nursing facility. And Mrs. Chen knew she was going somewhere, but didn't fully understand exactly where she was going and why. Because of her condition, she hadn't made many friends at the nursing home; so there were a few good-byes, but not many.

As she sat in the wheelchair, she wondered why they wouldn't let her walk out of this place. After all, she had walked into this place with her son, so even though he was gone, she should be able to walk out on her own.

"It's just the nursing home's policy," she was told.

It was a clear and sunny day, and Mrs. Chen could hear the birds singing as they rolled her toward the ambulance parked at the side of the nursing home.

Suddenly, a shot rang out!

"Someone's trying to kill me!" she screamed, as she bolted from her wheelchair and ran for cover.

The agents conducting the move quickly moved in to grab the culprit. Strangely enough, the shooter, the would-be assassin was just standing there across the street. He hadn't even thought of running. He was quickly apprehended. Later when he was tested for Covid-19, it turned out he was positive.

"This was supposed to be a suicide mission," he confessed, as he was handcuffed and escorted to a nearby undercover squad car by CIA operatives wearing face masks and latex gloves.

A news helicopter was first on the scene, soon to be followed by several news vans.

Later that night, as the news story was reported, those who read the on-air news speculated that this was more than likely a hate crime.

Jan and Jenny sat crossed legged on the floor in front of the television in Jenny's house.

"I wonder why they wanted to shoot such a nice old lady?" Jenny's mother asked.

Jan and Jenny said nothing. They were true to their promise. And they were afraid if anyone knew what they knew, that they would be next.

www.ingramcontent.com/pod-product-compliance
Ingram Content Group UK Ltd.
Pitfield, Milton Keynes, MK11 3LW, UK
UKHW020159200726
13856UKWH00003B/1073